LOUIE THE LOBSTER IN WHAT IS A FRIEND?

Story by: Sarah Gallant McCurdy & Arron J. McCurdy

Illustrations by: Kris Warden

Story by: Sarah Gallant McCurdy and Arron McCurdy
Illustrated by: Kris Warden

Note for Librarians: A cataloguing record for this book is available from Library and
Archives Canada at www.collectionscanada.ca/amicus/index-e.html
ISBN 978-0-9782955-0-9

Printed in Canada

Published by:
Crafty Canuck Inc.

Book sales for Canada, United States and International:

Order Online at:

http://www.louiethelobster.com

This book is for:

_____

and I would like to share it with my friend:

_____

As Louie "the Lobster" Bisque crawled up to the edge of North Rustico beach, he heard one top dweller say, "You always have the best time when you play with your friend. You should go outside and find your friend."

There were bad times, okay times, and once in awhile there was even a good time, but no sea creature had ever had the *best* time...until now. Louie knew that he had just found out what the secret to finding the *best* time is - a friend. One big problem: Louie had no idea what "a friend" was.

With the shallow beach waters heating up from the blazing sun and little bubbling beads of shiny sweat forming on Louie's top shell, he crawled around, slid down and got spun round all the way to his home at the bottom of the ocean, just off the coast of Prince Edward Island.

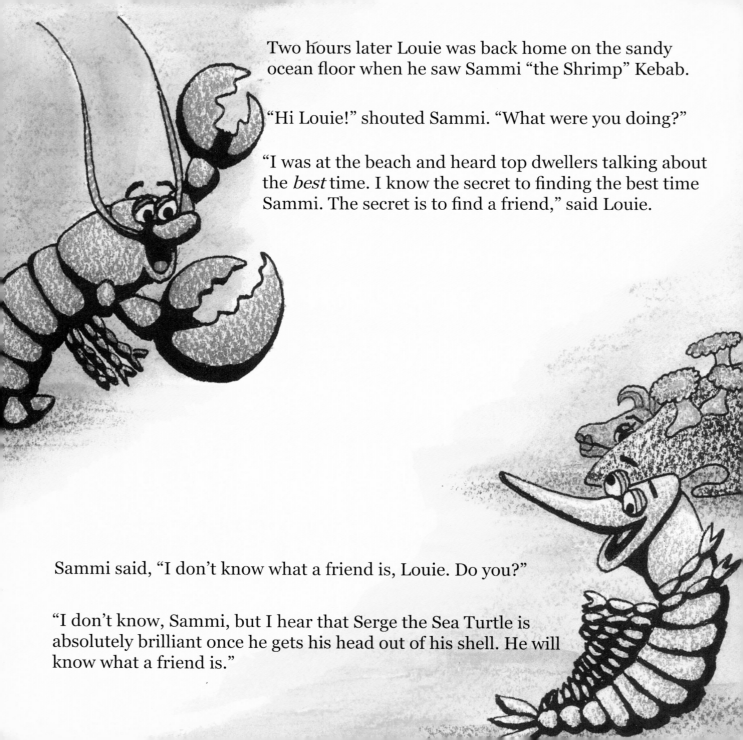

Two hours later Louie was back home on the sandy ocean floor when he saw Sammi "the Shrimp" Kebab.

"Hi Louie!" shouted Sammi. "What were you doing?"

"I was at the beach and heard top dwellers talking about the *best* time. I know the secret to finding the best time Sammi. The secret is to find a friend," said Louie.

Sammi said, "I don't know what a friend is, Louie. Do you?"

"I don't know, Sammi, but I hear that Serge the Sea Turtle is absolutely brilliant once he gets his head out of his shell. He will know what a friend is."

SWOOSH! SWOOSH! A brilliantly coloured school of fish zipped by from out of nowhere. "Look out!" cried Louie. "Watch out!" yelled the school of fish.

Just seconds before the crazy swimming school of fish was about to run over Sammi, Louie used his claws to pull Sammi safely out of the way.

"Wow! Sorry, Sammi," said the school of fish. "It is a good thing Louie was around to pull you out of our way or we may have hit you."

"Thank you, Louie! Next time I will look both ways when I hear a *SWOOSH! SWOOSH!*" panted Sammi.

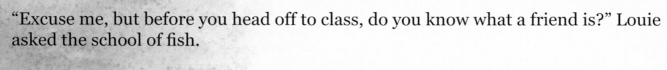

"Excuse me, but before you head off to class, do you know what a friend is?" Louie asked the school of fish.

"No, we're sorry, but we don't know what a friend is," apologized the school of fish. "We're late for class." *SWOOSH!* With a flick of their fine fins, the school of fish darted off before Louie and Sammi could say goodbye.

"Okay Sammi, let's keep going, but we must pay attention and be careful," warned Louie.

"Don't worry, Louie I will be careful. Come on, let's go!"

Continuing on their search they met Jag the Jellyfish, the biggest jellyfish Sammi and Louie had ever seen!

CLASS

"Jag the Jellyfish," asked Louie, "may Sammi and I jump on your jelly back?"

"Sure, climb aboard and jump away," invited Jag the Jellyfish.

"Louie, you go and play *jump-up* first," offered Sammi.

"I want us to play *jump-up* together," replied Louie.

Sammi and Louie climbed up and played *jump-up* together on Jag the Jellyfish.

"Thank you for letting us play with you Jag the Jellyfish. We had a super-duper time playing *jump-up*" they said together.

Since Sammi and Louie still did not know what a friend was, they kept heading toward Serge the Sea Turtle's home, until they came across a large, heavy-looking wooden box.

"Louie, Louie! Look over there. That box looks like it could be a million billion years old!" exclaimed Sammi. "Do you think there could be a friend inside?"

Sammi and Louie crawled quickly over to the large, heavy box that was at least a million billion years old. Louie took a few deep breaths and then tried to open the box with his claws. He grunted, groaned, and gurgled to the end but alas the lid would not bend.

"Sammi, I cannot open this box. I don't think I am strong enough to open it," said Louie as he struggled. His claws started to tremble and his teeth clinked and clanked as Louie pinched and poked at the lid of the large, heavy box.

"Move over, Louie. I will help you," said Sammi.

Louie and Sammi took a few moments to rest their muscles and then worked together to open the box. After one big push the heavy box that was at least a million billion years old opened up and let out a very loud *VRRRUUUMMMPHH.*

"Wow! It looks like we are stronger together!" exclaimed Louie.

"Come on, let's look inside for a friend," said Louie excitedly.

"Ah Louie, there is no friend in here, but there is a piece of super succulent saltwater seaweed!"

"It looks sooooo delicious," said Louie with a grin, as a little lobster juice dribbled down his chin.

"It doesn't look like we are ever going to find out what a friend is, Louie," said Sammi sadly.

"Oh yes we will, but first we will take a little break and enjoy this super succulent saltwater seaweed."

"Louie, there is only one piece in the box. Which one of us will get to enjoy this scrumptious piece of super succulent saltwater seaweed?" asked Sammi.

"I know what we'll do. We'll share this one piece," replied Louie.

Louie used his claws to cut the one piece of super succulent saltwater seaweed into TWO delicious pieces.

Sammi and Louie nestled into the ocean floor and started eating their pieces of the scrumptious seaweed.

"I'm glad we decided to share the piece of seaweed. That was very yummy," Sammi said gratefully.

"Yummy in my tummy," replied Louie. Both Sammi and Louie began to laugh.

"Look over there, just past the mussel farm, Sammi," said Louie. "That looks like Serge the Sea Turtle's house!"

Louie and Sammi crawled carefully past the mussel farm, trying hard not to disturb the mussels during their exercise time. One minute, two minutes, three minutes and just before minute four, Sammi and Louie reached the door.

"Bonjour," said Serge.

"Hello," replied Sammi and Louie. "Do you know what a friend is?"

"Bonjour?" replied Serge. Sammi and Louie turned to each other with puzzled looks on their faces.

"Sammi, I think Serge speaks only French. He may be the smartest sea turtle, but unless we start paying attention in French class, we will never find out what he is saying!"

As Sammi and Louie left Serge the Sea Turtle's home, they heard Serge say "Au revoir" and the door shut with a loud *SHUMPH*.

"What a day! We almost got knocked down by a crazy swimming school of fish, played *jump-up* with Jag the Jellyfish, worked together to open a big, million billion-year-old box, shared a piece of super succulent saltwater seaweed and met, but could not understand, Serge the Sea Turtle," said Sammi. "But we still don't know what a friend is!"

"Cheer up, Sammi! It's a big ocean out there. I'm sure someone can tell us what a friend is."

Just then, Ollie the Octopus came scooting by.

"Hello, Ollie," said Louie. "Sammi and I are searching to find out what a friend is. Do you know what a friend is?"

Ollie replied, "I cannot tell you exactly what a friend is, but I do know that you and Sammi are friends."

Sammi said, "I'm a shrimp, not a friend."

"Yes, I'm a lobster, not a friend," agreed Louie.

"No, I'm telling the truth. I heard Elly the Eel say, 'Louis et Sammi sont des bons amis' to Serge the Sea Turtle.

I wish I could have stayed longer to hear more, but I was rushing the fish to swim class," explained Ollie the Octopus.

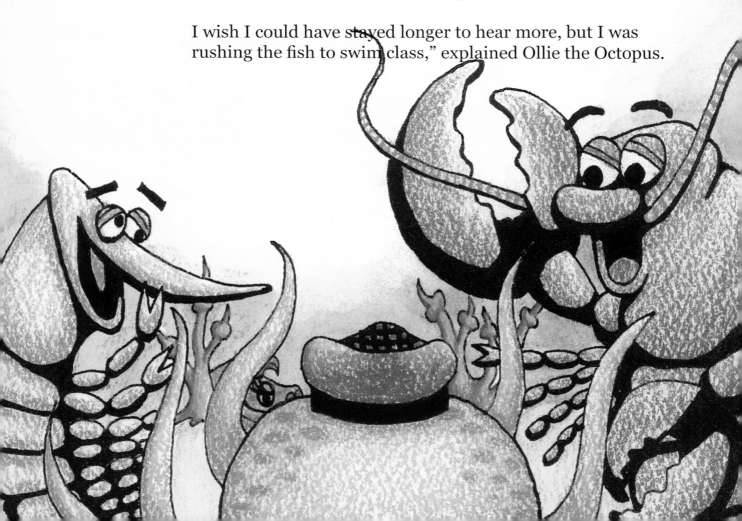

Before Louie and Sammi could ask Ollie what "Louis et Sammi sont des bons amis" meant in English, Ollie gave them a two-tentacled wave goodbye.

"Boy Louie, we really need to start paying attention in French class," said Sammi.

"Let's go find Elly the Eel. She has to know what a friend is," insisted Louie.

Sammi and Louie eagerly crawled on to find Elly the Eel when suddenly, she appeared in front of them.

"Hello, Sammi and Louie. It's nice to see you two out this way," said Elly.

"Ollie told us we are friends," Louie explained to Elly. "Are we friends?" he asked.

"Yes. I was just telling Serge the Sea Turtle that you and Sammi are good friends," replied Elly.

"But I don't understand," Sammi said, puzzled. "What is a friend?"

"I am sure that you are friends. I have been watching you. Find a soft spot on the ocean floor and I'll try to explain this to you both," said Elly.

Elly explained, "Remember when you pulled Sammi away from the crazy swimming school of fish, Louie? That is what a friend does."

"Remember when you played *jump-up* together on Jag the Jellyfish? That is what friends do."

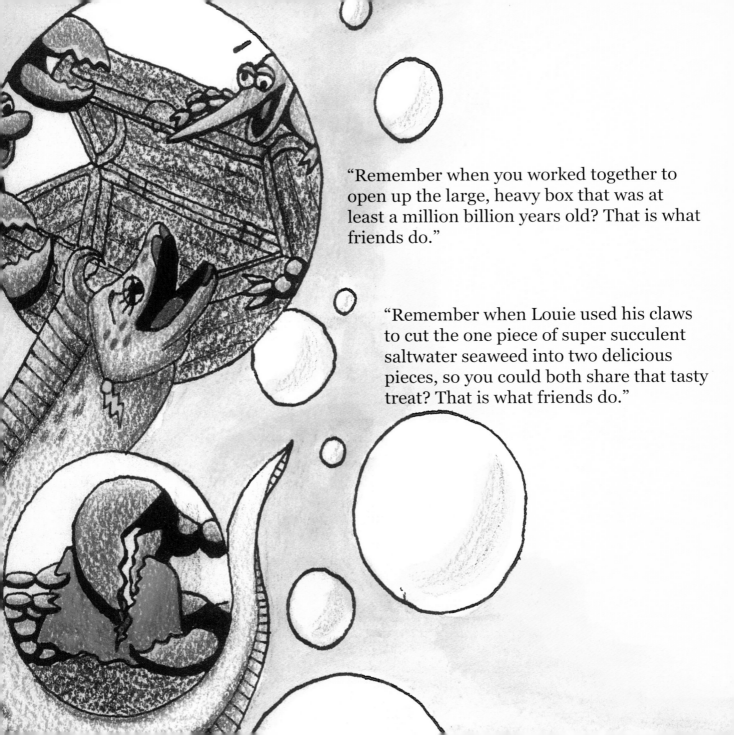

"Remember when you worked together to open up the large, heavy box that was at least a million billion years old? That is what friends do."

"Remember when Louie used his claws to cut the one piece of super succulent saltwater seaweed into two delicious pieces, so you could both share that tasty treat? That is what friends do."

"Remember cheering each other up when you thought you would never find out what a friend was after meeting with Serge the Sea Turtle?" asked Elly. "That is what friends do."

"You two are friends. That is for sure."

Together, Sammi and Louie said: "Wow, we are friends."

"Friends protect each other."

"And share."

"And help each other."

"And care."

"You and I will always be friends!" said Louie.

"Elly, now that Sammi and I know we are friends, how do we have the *best* time?"

"Oh, that's easy," replied Elly, "any time you spend with your friend will always be the *best* time."

Happy to be friends, Louie and Sammi scuttled across the ocean floor in search of their next adventure together.

"PSST...Yes, you. It's me, Sammi. Have you seen Louie?

I have looked everywhere for him but he just disappeared. We were playing yesterday and were
supposed to meet up today at the elevator farm but he didn't show up.

Do you know where he is?

If you see Louie, please let me know."

Find out what happens to Louie in his next adventure:

One Claw Short